For Timothy ~ J. E.
For Hugo, Ellie, and Douglas ~ V. C.

Text © 2008 by Jonathan Emmett
Illustrations © 2008 by Vanessa Cabban

First U.S. edition 2008

Library of Congress Cataloging-in-Publication Data is available.

Library of Congress Catalog Card Number pending

ISBN 978-0-7636-3860-3

2 4 6 8 10 9 7 5 3 1

Printed in Singapore

This book was typeset in Beta Bold.
The illustrations were done in watercolor and pencil.

Candlewick Press
2067 Massachusetts Avenue
Cambridge, Massachuetts 02140

visit us at www.candlewick.com

The Best Gift of All

Jonathan Emmett

illustrated by Vanessa Cabban

CANDLEWICK PRESS
CAMBRIDGE, MASSACHUSETTS

"HOT-DIGGETY DRAT!" said Mole,
poking his head out of the ground one morning.
"It's raining AGAIN!"

Mole did not like going out in the rain.
"The only place to be in this weather
is underground," he said.

But it had been raining all week, and Mole
was missing his friends—especially Rabbit.
Mole hadn't seen her for days, and he was
beginning to worry about her.

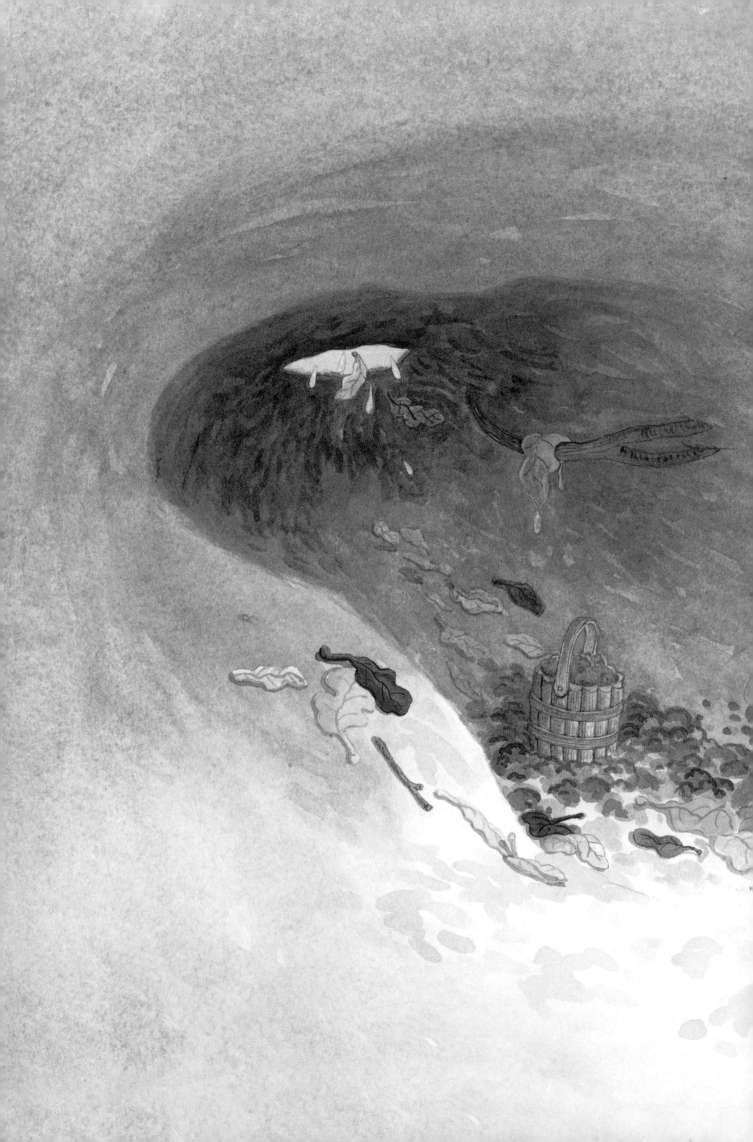

"Dear Rabbit," Mole said with a sigh.
"It would be so nice to see her."

And then Mole had a wonderful idea.

"I don't need to go out in the rain
to see Rabbit," Mole told himself.
"I can visit her BY TUNNEL!"

And he began to dig.

Squirrel had been
collecting nuts
beneath the shelter
of the trees

and was about
to bury them.

Squirrel dropped the nuts into a hole
and then jumped back in surprise as
"Ouch!
Ouch!
Ouch!"
cried a voice from below.

Squirrel peered down the hole
and was astonished to see Mole
peering back up at her.

"Mole!" said Squirrel.
"What are you doing
at the bottom of my hole?"

"Squirrel!" said Mole with a laugh.
"What are you doing
at the top of my tunnel?"

Mole explained that he was going
to see Rabbit.

"What a great idea," said Squirrel.
"Can I come too?"

Hedgehog had
found a pile
of dry leaves

and had just
settled down
for a nap

when he felt
something scrape
his backside.

"What the weevil?"
he cried, leaping
to his feet.

"Sorry, Hedgehog," said Mole,
appearing out of the ground. "I came up
to find a way around these roots."

"We're off to see Rabbit," cried Squirrel,
popping her head out of the tunnel.

"We haven't seen her for days," said Mole.

"What a splendid idea," said Hedgehog.
"Can I come too?"

It was dark in the tunnel, and neither Squirrel nor Hedgehog was used to being underground. All they could do was follow Mole.

"How can you tell where we are?"
asked Squirrel.

"Are you sure we're going the right way?"
asked Hedgehog.

"Don't worry," Mole assured them.
"If there's one thing I'm good at,
it's digging tunnels."

Rabbit lay in her burrow
feeling miserable.
She had a terrible cold
and was staying inside
until the weather got better.
But it had been raining all week,
and she was missing her friends—especially Mole.
She was worried that they might have forgotten her.

It's so lonely stuck here on my own,
she thought. *It would be lovely*
if someone dropped
in to see me.

Just then there was a scrabbling sound,
and a lump of earth fell from the burrow ceiling.

And before Rabbit could take a closer look,
there was a shower of soil, and Mole, Hedgehog,
and Squirrel dropped, one after another,
onto the burrow floor.

"Mole! Squirrel! Hedgehog!" said Rabbit, smiling.
"I was just thinking how much
I missed you."

When Mole, Squirrel,
and Hedgehog realized
that Rabbit was under the weather,
they couldn't stop fussing over her.
Squirrel went back down the tunnel
and brought Rabbit some of her nuts to eat,
and Hedgehog fetched some of his dry leaves
to make a fresh bed.

And it wasn't long before Rabbit
was feeling better
and chatting happily.

Only Mole looked unhappy.

"What's wrong, Mole?" Rabbit asked.

"Everyone has brought something to make
you feel better," explained Mole,
"except ME—and I'VE missed
you the most!"

"Oh, Mole," said Squirrel.

"YOU shouldn't feel bad. After all,
it was YOUR idea to visit Rabbit."

"And we would never have gotten here,"
agreed Hedgehog, "without YOUR tunnel."

"And you DID bring me something . . .
or someone," said Rabbit.

Mole grinned when he realized what Rabbit meant.
"I brought you your FRIENDS!" he said.

"Yes," said Rabbit, "you brought me my friends.
And that's the
BEST GIFT OF ALL."